SEBASTIAN'S MONSTER

Tanya Popovski

PoP-O Books
Deepening Understanding

Published by PoP-O Books 2018

www.popobooks.com.au

Copyright © 2018 Tanya Popovski

Illustrations by Chris McQuinlan

http://chrismacquinlanart.artstation.com

A catalogue record for this book is available from the National Library of Australia.

Book cover design and formatting services by BookCoverCafe.com

First edition 2018

ISBN 978-0-6482019-3-9 (pbk)

ACKNOWLEDGEMENTS

Thank you to my nephew, Isaac, for being the first to trial my educational resource. His ability to express his thoughts assisted me in further developing and refining the way in which I would ask the questions.

And a huge thank-you to my two children, who armed me with material for my stories.

ONE night, Sebastian called out, 'Mum, Dad, I can't sleep, there's a monster in my room.'

Sebastian's room was filled with toys. Bears, Lego, dinosaurs and toy trucks lined his shelves.

Every night, Sebastian's parents came in before sleep time to say goodnight.

Either Mum or Dad read Sebastian a story, gave him a kiss on the cheek and switched off the light as they left the room.

Mum came back into the room and asked Sebastian calmly, 'What does this monster look like?'

'Well, I'm not sure. It was dark, and I didn't get to see it clearly.'

'Did it tell you its name?' Mum asked.

'No,' Sebastian said, feeling confused. He was hoping his mum would say there were no such things as monsters.

'Does it have little ears?' Mum queried.

'Maybe,' said Sebastian.

'And does it have big feet?'

'I don't know,' said Sebastian.

Sebastian forgot how scared he'd been.

He was stunned that his mum knew so much about the monster.

'So, Mum, do you actually believe that I had a monster in my room?' Sebastian asked in a squeaky voice.

'Yes, I do, and I think I might know exactly who is in your room. When I was a little girl, Scooty used to come and wish me goodnight. At first I didn't know why he came, and I was just as scared as you.'

'Who was Scooty?' Sebastian asked.

And so Sebastian's mum told him the story of Scooty.

'When I was your age, I used to hold my doll tightly when I was trying to fall asleep,' Mum said. 'Sometimes I would see a monster in my room. I'd call out to my parents, just like you did, but as soon as they came into my room the monster always vanished.'

'My parents used to comfort me and tuck me in, give me a kiss and tell me it was just my imagination,' Mum said.

'What did you do?' Sebastian asked his mum.

'I devised a plan. I started leaving a little pile of biscuits beside my wardrobe. I knew that if the monster started eating them I'd be able to talk to it. It would be too busy munching on the biscuits to munch on me.'

'The next
night, as soon as
my parents left my room,
I took out the bag of biscuits that
I'd been hiding all day. They were all
crumbly by then, but I didn't worry about
that. I put out the biscuits and crept back into
bed. My room was dark and silent.'

'Were you scared?' Sebastian asked.

'Yes, a little bit,' she said. 'My fear had started
to creep up inside me, but I was determined to
push it away and carry out my plan. I heard
a rustling sound near my wardrobe. I took
out my torch and turned it on. There stood
a giant blue and furry creature. It had tiny
ears on the sides of its round head, and
its feet looked like flippers. It didn't look
that scary at all.'

'The furry creature told me that his name was Scooty,' Mum said, 'and Scooty and I had a long talk together.'

'What did you talk about?' Sebastian asked.

'He told me that it was his job to look after me, and he hadn't meant to scare me. So every night after that, after my parents had said goodnight and turned off the light, I said goodnight to Scooty. I felt safe and secure, knowing that Scooty was there looking after me, and I always slept soundly.'

After hearing his mum's story, Sebastian felt a lot calmer and happier.

But he wasn't totally convinced that his mum's monster was the same monster as his monster, so he devised a plan ...

ABOUT THE AUTHOR

TANYA POPOVSKI has a Bachelor of Education from the University of Wollongong, and over twenty-five years of teaching experience working with primary school-aged children. She is also a mother of two children. Tanya's experience moves beyond the classroom and into the realms of special education, behaviour support, literacy support, NAPLAN analysis, and development and training in the area of Focus on Reading.

Tanya's passion is educating children to be the best that they can be. She understands the key role that parents play in their child's education as the first educators in their child's life. Giving parents access to explicit teaching and good questioning can only have a positive impact on their child's learning, by being exposed daily to the process of analysing, synthesising and evaluating texts. With these skills, children will be better equipped to apply these thinking skills to any text within a subject area.

PoP-O Books offers a way to explicitly teach important comprehension skills through discussion. Annotated questions and answers help to target questions found in NAPLAN.

Learn with

Previous title by Tanya Popovski

Amelia Faces Her Anxiety

(picture book + question guide)

Everyone feels some level of anxiety at different times,
and Amelia is no different.

She wants to go on year 5's overnight trip, but she's
very worried about it.

What will she do?

Will she face her anxiety or give in to it?

New title coming soon

Cranky Corey

(picture book + question guide)

Everyone knows someone like Corey.

When things don't go to plan during sporting games,
he always throws tantrums and storms off the field.

Will Corey's friends tell him the truth about his behaviour?

Will he accept responsibility for his tantrums?

Each title includes:

- Reader's storybook

- Annotated storybook with questions and answers

- Tracking sheet linked to the Australian curriculum

  (sold separately at www.popobooks.com.au)

Mid-Upper Primary

Running Words 626
Text Type: Narrative

PoP-O Books
Deepening Understanding